Just a Game

Amenemopé McKinney

To the game, my best friend, my greatest teacher, my first love and the love of my life

CONTENTS

ACKNOWLEDGMENTS

Thank you Jesus Christ for being my savior. Lord, I told you if you gave me the words I would write the book. Thank you for guiding me. This belongs to you. Bless it and allow it to be a blessing to others.

I want to thank my parents, Damitia Boyd-McKinney and Gregory McKinney, for always believing in me and encouraging me to never be satisfied with mediocre. I want to thank my mom for being my support system and always being someone I could count on. I know everything you had to sacrifice for my sister and me and for this I am grateful. I want to thank my dad for wanting what is best for me. I'd like to say thank you to my younger sister, Nzingha, for making me laugh and for making me so proud to be your big sister. No one will ever be able to take your place. I want to thank the matriarchs of my family, my grandmother, Willie Ruth Boyd and the "Golden Girls" (Geraldine Lewis, Katie Greene, Grace Graham, and Evelyn Bonner). You ladies are beautiful queens and I am inspired daily by you.

I'd like to say thank you to all of the

coaches – Greg Williams, Jae Cross, Rebecca Kates-Taylor, Kim Austin, Carlos Quintero, Wanda Talton, Ray DeBord, Diana DeBord, Dennis Harris, Kelly Carruthers, Shaka Massey and Tim Miller - I have played for over the years. You pushed me not only to be a better basketball player but you pushed me to be a better person. Your lessons really stuck with me and if I didn't understand it then, I get it now. Thank you.

Thank you to my teammates; I've learned just as much from you as I've learned from our coaches. I've played alongside some great players who have become even greater friends. I know that you will always have my back. Thank you.

Thank you to all of my mentors – Kevin Caldwell, Brittani Rettig, Chason Crosby, Maudess Fulton - who always tell me the truth and set great examples for me. Thanks for putting up with all of my crazy ideas which because of you I don't think are all that crazy anymore.

I want to say thank you to all of my friends and family for your love and support over the years. I'm truly grateful to have you in my corner. I think I have the greatest friends and family in the entire world.

Thank you to my players and their parents for allowing me to be your coach. Coaching you all is a great privilege and I do not take it lightly. I pray that I have a positive impact on your life. You all bring me many smiles and laughs. You are beautiful, intelligent and gifted young ladies. I know you all will do great things. You make me better.

Lastly, I would like to thank the game. You have taken me places I never thought I would go. You have introduced me to some of my best friends. I honestly didn't think I would still be playing and I never thought I would coach. For whatever reason, I still love you and I just can't let go.

PROLOUGE

The very first time I met the game, I knew it would change my life. But even then, I didn't fully realize the magnitude by which it would affect me. Back then, I thought it was just a game. Today, if you were to tell me that basketball is just a game, there is no way we could be friends. The game is my best friend—and some days, it feels like it's my only friend. When everything else is wrong, the game is still right. I never had to try with the game. It came effortlessly—until it didn't. The game evolved and I with it. But growth doesn't come without pain. Even on bad days, the game never had to convince me to show up. I've known the game for as long as I can remember, and it's hard to imagine a life in which the game doesn't exist. Over the years, I haven't found anything comparable to the game. I guess you could say ball is life.

Part 1

1 BIG TIME PLAYERS

My coach called a timeout. There were only 32 seconds left in what had turned out to be the greatest AAU basketball game of the summer. When the game began the gym was hot, with the kind of dry heat that you'd expect in a desert. However, as the game went on, the air became thick with the humidity that comes from too many bodies being too close together. A giant industrial-sized fan spun in the corner, but its breeze was blocked by fans trying to cool themselves off. It was an unusually large gym— much larger than most high school gyms—and it was packed. It was so crowded that people were standing in the doorway to watch. If I didn't know any better, I would have thought Kobe were in the gym. After all, people didn't usually turn out like this for girls' basketball games. But this was different. There were people on top of people on top of people. I think people passing through the gym had to notice how tight the game was, and the game schedule for the main court may have been behind, but anyone who was here on accident was now here for this game. They picked a team, and everyone was cheering. Maybe it was the heat. Maybe it was the atmosphere. Maybe it was the closeness of the score and the back and forth of it. Maybe it was the proximity to other fans. Maybe it was the energy of the coaches. Maybe it was the intensity of the teams. Or just maybe, having all of these things mixed together was what told me that the game was indeed a classic.

As we were walking back out onto the court at the end of the timeout, my coach (aka my dad) pulled me to the side. "Mackenzie," he said, "big time players show up in big time games." This was something he had told me a thousand times before. It felt strange for him to be telling me again now, because I thought I *was* living up to the moment. #32 and I had gone back and forth the whole fourth quarter, all leading up to this very moment. When we walked out onto the court, I looked at #32 and she looked at me with the respect that only comes from great competition. She had given me her best, and I had given her mine.

The other team had possession of the ball. #32 received the ball on the inbounds as expected, and she dribbled around wasting time. I moved up to guard her tight, and she made a move to the right—the same one she had been killing me on all game, but this time I anticipated it. She countered and pulled up for a jump shot. I fouled her. Two shots. The score was 63–64 in our favor. I ran over to my coach, feeling slightly defeated and ever more conscious of what this moment meant. Again he tells me, "Big time players show up in big time games. Forget what just happened. Be in the moment. It is yours. There are 12 seconds left. Finish strong."

#32 hit both free throws. 65–64. We were down by one point with 12 seconds left on the clock and no timeouts remaining. My teammate inbounded the ball to me by rolling it to keep the clock stopped. #32 ran up to make a play on the ball, so I picked up the ball and began dribbling. 11…10…9…8. As I crossed half court, I locked eyes with my 6'4 teammate, Rachel. The look she gave me said it all: We both knew *exactly* what time it was. I dribbled to the right side of the court, only to quickly change directions and come back left. It was obvious to me that #32 had no idea what was coming when she ran into that 6'4 brick wall. I came off of Rachel's screen, with a hard switch to the left. I could hear my teammates from the bench counting down, 5…4…3…2. I got all the way to the rim and finished with my left hand as I was fouled by a defender that was late on the help rotation. The back board turned red, signaling that the clock had expired. The score was 65–66: We had won. My teammate Rachel came and gave me a giant hug. "Rachel," I told her, "we won because of you!"

"I know Kenzie," she said, "I know."

After the game, the gym was on fire with excitement. Even after the sportsmanship handshakes and the coaches' huddles, both teams lingered. Everyone felt it: Something special had just taken place. Soon enough, my mom found me, and she was smiling from ear to ear. It was the kind of my smile that lets a kid know their mom is proud—and that they could have whatever they want for dinner later. I already knew exactly what I wanted, too: lasagna, broccoli, mashed potatoes, and garlic toast. I could taste the lasagna, already. God bless my mother for that meal.

My boyfriend, Bryce, was the next to find

me. At about 6'2 with short hair and an athletic build, he was the perfect height to complement my 5'9 frame. He was always well dressed, and his life was just like his wardrobe: very much in order. He already knew he was going to go to Easton University in Pennsylvania on a full academic scholarship. He was probably going to be the next African American to win a Nobel Peace Prize. He was that smart and that determined. Every day for the last year and a half I had wondered how I ended up dating a guy like him. I mean, I was smart and everything. I made straight A's in school and was in the top 10% of my class, but I was really all about basketball. I didn't know where I was going to college because I was just waiting on the right basketball scholarship offer. I had received a few offers, but I was waiting on something bigger to come my way. He often urged me to just go the academic route—I had been offered a scholarship to Easton, too, he would point out.

"There is so much more to life than this game, Kenzie" Bryce would say. Some days, I almost believed him.

2 NO LIMITS

Before I knew it, the scholarship I had been waiting for came around November of my senior year of high school. Off I went to Turner University in New York to play basketball and continue my education. From that point on, my entire mindset shifted. I was on a mission to be the best. I felt like owed that to the game that was taking me to college.

Throughout my senior year of high school, I trained like never before, realizing that this new level of competition would require new levels of sacrifice. No one seemed to understand my dedication to preparation, other than my best friend Carter Reyes. Carter pushed me harder than any coach I'd ever had. Carter, a basketball player himself, had blown out his knee just before our senior year in high school, ending his basketball career prematurely. He could play pick up, although his doctor would probably faint if he found out Carter was playing. Carter was just that kind of guy. He made his own rules, and his self-confidence was infectious to those around him.

This Tuesday we played pick-up for about three hours with grown men—men who took pride in not giving the young lady on the court anything free. After the game, Carter suggested that I run ten sprints. His tone suggested it was more of a demand than a suggestion. "Mackenzie," he said, "you got this. No problem." I replied, "C-Rey, are you trying to kill me?" At the moment, I was sure he was. I had no legs left after having run eleven straight games with minimal breaks in between. This was my last day at home before leaving for my first semester of school at Turner. I just wanted to rest and relax for the remainder of the day, feeling good about going undefeated in my last runs at home. C-Rey and I always ran the court if we were on the same team.

In typical fashion, Carter shrugged and pulled his stopwatch from his street shoes. I walked up to the line and prepared to run the ten sprints that would end my life. So much for

Turner University. The first five sprints went fairly easy. Sprint number six came with a little more of a challenge. I was winded. I felt my mind and my energy waning, and all I could think about was what we were going to have for dinner. Lord Jesus, I was going to miss my mother's cooking. After sprint seven, the burn in my legs started to intensify. I asked for a few extra seconds of rest. Of course, that was a no-go. Sprint eight came and went. I barely made my time, and everything in the room was becoming blurry. My ears were popping, and the sound of the other guys talking in the gym became jumbled and faded. My mind said no way you can do number nine, and my body told me death was imminent if I somehow made it to number ten. I don't know how I carried the weight of my body to do sprint nine, but I knew sprint ten was out of the question when I tasted bile in my mouth.

I stepped away from the line in desperate search of a trash can to take care of what I knew was coming. As I stood slumped over the trash can, Carter, who at this point was my least favorite person in the world, came up to me and whispered in my ear, "there are no limits for you other than the ones you create for yourself, and I'm about to show you. Get back on the line, you have one less second for this last rep starting in 5,

4, 3…" His voice trailed off as I locked in and walked back to the line to push through every doubt that I had. I got down in the ready position, drenched in sweat, muscles I didn't know I had screaming at me, and my hands and feet tingling.

"Go!"

I sprinted as though my life depended on it. I felt like I was running to the white light. When I crossed the line, my legs buckled, and I fell to ground. Every fiber of my body was furious at me. If I were to pour gasoline on my head and set myself on fire, this might be what it felt like. Hands over my head, out of breath, and hoping I had made my time, I suddenly became aware of my surroundings again. Carter was standing over me, screaming, jumping, and hitting me with a huge smile. I don't know why he was so happy, since he obviously needed to be seeking medical attention for me. Whatever he was saying he kept repeating it until my hearing returned and his words finally registered.

"8.6 seconds, Kenzie. 8.6 seconds!" I couldn't believe it. If he was saying what I thought, he was saying this would be the fastest I'd ever run the last sprint of the day. Under the circumstances, I needed to see the watch for myself. In that moment, it seemed like the whole gym stopped—but I knew everyone was watching us. We celebrated as if we had just won the lottery. I had no idea where this surge of energy came from, but I was hyped up, jumping and dancing. I think it was part adrenaline from the sprints and part excitement from achieving a personal best, but it was mostly trying to savor these last moments with my best friend, knowing no one else would ever push me the way he just had—and that no one would ever believe in me the way he did. It's so sad that this friendship would need to come to an end, but that seemed to be what everyone was telling me. Once you go to college, your high school friends grow apart.

On the drive home, in Carter's 2006 black Toyota Corolla, Carter couldn't stop talking about the new level we had just achieved. All he kept telling me was to promise him that every time my new coach, Coach Daniels, asked me to run another sprint or do another rep in the weight room or stay in the game despite extreme fatigue, all things which I thought were humanly impossible at the time, to remember that there truly are no limits. He told me to just keep the love of the game with me, and there would be no limits on or off the court.

I stopped believing in limits that day. I understand that limits don't really exist. At one time, I knew this only in the context of the game. But now the game was inside of me. Everything that I only felt empowered to do by the game, I now feel empowered to do in every aspect of my life. The game made me stronger. The game made me feel invincible. Before the game, I felt powerless and without an identity. But now, I understood the love of the game and that the love of the game exists beyond the four lines on the court—which made me powerful beyond limits.

3 STRIVE FOR GREATNESS

Move-in day at Turner University was both exciting and strange all at the same time. Thousands of new faces in this grand new place. It was a hot August day that no one wanted to end. Turner was unlike any place I'd ever been before. The campus was green and vast. The trees were tall and majestic. The buildings were a mixture of ancient and modern architecture, all posturing in a way that was pristine. Walking through campus I was a bit in awe that this would be where I would spend the next four years of my life. I could tell that I wasn't the only freshmen at Turner that was ready to take the campus by storm. My mom, my dad, my older brother Kameron, and Bryce all came to drop me off at my new home.

Three of the upper classmen from the basketball team, Lauren Grater, aka "LG," Tyesha Hobbs aka "Ty," and Kaylen Brown along with the coaches greeted my family and Bryce, helping us move into my new dorm room. Kaylen didn't have a nickname yet, because I didn't know her all that well. Every time I visited campus for games she was standoffish. Even then, she didn't seem like she really wanted to be there.

Moving into my room didn't take nearly as long as expected, thanks to all of the extra help from my teammates and coaches. After we finished, Bryce and my family wanted to take me to dinner. I was tired and in dire need of a nap after all of the moving. While I didn't want them to leave, I was eager to make new friends and meet up with my teammates later that night. I didn't know the next time I'd get to see Bryce or my family, so I found the energy and the will to say yes.

At dinner, my dad went into coach mode. He never really knew how to separate the two, being a father and being a coach. He had been coaching me since the time I was a five year old, playing at the YMCA, up until now. He wouldn't dare let anyone else coach his kids. He started his coaching career when Kam started showing signs at a young age that he could be good. Over the years, Dad had become infamous for pulling out the clipboard to discuss plays over dinner or wanting to watch game film instead of going to the movies. Almost every conversation with him came back to basketball and what I needed to do better to get to the next level. He was a great coach, and much of my success I can attribute to him. But sometimes I didn't need a coach—I just needed a dad. I hated not knowing how to tell him.

At the conclusion of his dissertation about how I needed to stick to my diet of no sweets and soda in college, he reached into his pocket and pulled out a long black velvet box. I looked over at Bryce, who had become restless in his seat. He nodded as if to say he knew nothing about this. My dad was not a random gift type of guy. He just wasn't built that way. He handed me the box with the biggest smile on his face. I opened it with caution, feeling slightly nervous. Inside the box was a silver chain with a silver basketball locket. I opened the locket. Inside there was a simple inscription: "Strive for Greatness."

"Thanks, Dad! This is beautiful," I said with a mixture of excitement and apprehension, unsure whether or not to get up and hug him.

You give big bear hugs to dads when they do this sort of thing, right? I thought to myself. But then again, this was a gift from my coach, and there were boundaries. I decided I loved the necklace so much that I didn't care about the boundaries and leapt up to give my father a hug. I would miss him. I'd miss my dad, and I'd miss my coach.

Bryce interrupted what almost could have been a genuine father-daughter moment with a question to my dad as he inspected my new necklace. "Strive for greatness—what does that mean to you, Coach Moore?" Everyone called my dad Coach Moore. He liked that. Mr. Moore was severely frowned upon.

"Striving for greatness means never be satisfied. Greatness is an ideal—and an elusive one at that. Greatness cannot be easily obtained. If being great were easy, everyone would be great. It's true that everyone wants to be great, but the vast majority of the population is average. They go with the crowd, they do the minimum, and they are complacent," he paused to gather his thoughts, "Striving is to constantly reach for a goal and to constantly fight against your natural inclinations to give up when results don't come quickly," said my father, never sounding more like a coach.

Bryce, always loving a philosophical discussion, replied, "That all makes sense. I'd also add that you can't strive for greatness in anything that you don't have passion for. I think it's the passion that drives you to keep fighting when you don't feel like it."

Kam and my mom were both staring at me, pleading me to stop the madness before it started. My dad and Bryce could both talk with the best of them. I could tell my dad's gift made Kam feel a certain level of disappointment. Kam, four years my senior, the golden child of the family, had since fallen out of the good graces of our father. My dad was always taking shots at Kam for turning down the opportunity to go pro in order to start a sports analytics company with a couple of his college buddies. My dad had called Kam every name in the book, and had even made up some new ones, when he found out. Dad didn't talk to anybody for weeks. It was like Kam had ripped out his heart and squeezed it until there was absolutely no life left in it. Ball was never Kam's dream even though he was one of the best players I'd ever seen. The pressure put on Kam was always too much. After my dad recovered from Kam's supposed betrayal, I got all of dad's attention. The weight of his hopes and dreams transferred to me. The difference between

Kam and I was that I played the game because I truly loved it. Kam had only played to earn dad's respect and love.

Kam told me how he knew he shouldn't go pro by saying, "I was just in love with the accolades, the applause and the attention. I hated showing up every day. I didn't work hard, I just had talent, and Dad is a hell of a trainer. When there were no accolades or attention to be had, I hated basketball. I hated practice, I hated conditioning, I hated every single minute of it. I was an attention junkie. And if you only do it because you yearn for the attention, you are an attention junkie, too. But if you are in love with the grind, in love with the process, in love with the work and can show up when no one is there to cheer for you, then you are truly in love with the game."

I jumped into the conversation, hoping to redirect it before it became too late. "Dad, thank you for this. It means a lot to me. I promise you, I will strive for greatness daily. I commit to it." I committed to it with the full knowledge that my dad was going to hold me to every word. Accountability was a really big deal for my dad. I could already hear him two months from now: "On August 16th, at 7:53 PM, you committed to striving for greatness." That was his way. So I didn't make the commitment half-heartedly. That day, I committed to give my all. Every achievement would be a step, not a destination. Every obstacle would be a bridge to go over, under, or through—and if that failed, I'd burn it down. I was going to give my all in this next journey of my life. I had resigned to the fact that I probably could never truly make my dad proud. But I was going to be proud of myself, because I was going to honor my commitment and give my all to the game that I loved. And when my all seemingly wasn't enough, I would find more to give.

4 YOU GET WHAT YOU PAY FOR

August passed very quickly, and September followed suit. I was beginning to miss my family. Bryce came to visit a few times, which was nice. The distance was definitely straining our relationship, mainly because he didn't understand all that went along with being a division one collegiate athlete.

In two short months, I'd watched the game change from something unrestricted and free to something formalized and corporate. The game grew up from Nike flip-flops and backpacks to Turner polos and suit cases. College athletics was like a marriage, and every action came within the confines of that marriage. There was study hall, recruiting, donor dinners, professional development, and community service. You were ultimately accountable to the team and most of your time was dedicated to team activities. And then there was all the baggage that came with your nuptial to the game. I could see the love-hate relationship that the upper classmen had with the game. I couldn't help but wonder if the same thing would happen to me.

Bryce frequently complained that I didn't have time for him anymore. I think he believed I was cheating on him. He would say that I was not showing him enough attention. He wanted to talk and text 24/7, which wasn't possible with the schedule I had. My days were fully committed to the game. My schedule started at five in the morning and often didn't conclude until after ten o'clock in the evening. When he came to visit, he saw firsthand that I was stretched thin and could barely keep my own schedule. He tried to be supportive, but I knew it wasn't genuine. He was used to being the center of attention, and at this point in my life, that was something I couldn't give him.

At night, I no longer dreamed about Bryce but was instead haunted by the face of Coach Daniels, whistle in his mouth yelling for the team to get back on the line. I was perpetually afraid of being late for a workout and could never get a good night's rest the night before an early work out. I wasn't alone in my stress, either: The two other freshmen on the team, Stephanie Miles and Rene Townsend, echoed the same sentiment. We were three weeks into practice, and we were forced to learn quickly. The grind of practice had my body constantly aching in pain. Frequent ice baths saved my body from completely falling apart, and the upper classmen told me it would only get worse once the season began. Coach Daniels' favorite thing to tell us over the last few weeks was, "You get what you pay for!" I think it was just his way of justifying his sadistic love of suicides, a conditioning drill in which we had to run down the court and touch a different line each time. I swear, he grinned every time he sent us to the line.

The night before our first practice, we had a team dinner at Coach Daniels' house. His wife cooked a magnificent meal. It was the first home-cooked food I had eaten in months. I ate like I hadn't seen food in years and went back for seconds and then thirds. The cafeteria food was decent, but it couldn't touch my mom's cooking. God bless my mother. I spoke to her every day. She would tell me what she was cooking for dinner that day, and I could taste the macaroni and cheese or steak right on the tip of my tongue right before it disappeared like a mirage.

After dinner, the team and the coaches sat outside around a toasty fire pit in Coach Daniels' backyard. It was the type of team bonding that didn't feel forced. We all went around the circle, sharing our team goals for the season. There was consensus among the team that our first goal was to win the conference title. The next goal was to win a national championship. Coach urged us to put all of our effort toward the first goal. Only once that goal was accomplished could we then put our effort toward the second goal. We set several smaller goals, too. Coach Daniels demanded excellence in the classroom as well, giving us a team goal of a 3.0 GPA.

Coach Daniels never missed an opportunity to remind us of the theme of the season: You get what you pay for. If we wanted to achieve our goals, we had to first pay the price. Achieving greatness did not come easy, nor was it cheap. There is a price that you have to pay to be great. There are sacrifices that you have to make along the way to achieve greatness. He asked if we were willing to pay the price. We all said yes, but at the time I don't think we fully grasped what that meant.

Things that come free or easy are enticing,

but they simply don't last. The saying is "easy come, easy go." However, the things that you are willing to work for, the things that you put every fiber of your being into, the things you earn— those are the things that will last. You value things that you work for more than things that are given to you. It hurts more when you lose when you have consistently put the work in. But it is also that much sweeter when you win because you know all the work you did in the dark when no one was watching.

Everyone wants to be like someone else they perceive to be great, but they do not necessarily understand what that person went through to be great. They don't see the personal struggles they deal with that come along with the fame or the money.

I felt the sacrifice in the constant aching pain in my body. I felt the sacrifice in my relationship with Bryce. I felt the sacrifice when I could hear the parties on campus and I was in my room studying. Classes were kicking my tail, which was new for me. School had always come easy to me—up until now.

5 YOU MUST BE PRESENT TO WIN

It was the day of our first game. The game was at home, against Rochester State University. The night before the game I couldn't sleep. I think it was a mixture of nerves and outside distractions. I took a run around the campus at about three o'clock in the morning, which had become my nightly custom. There had been a lot on my mind lately with my father in and out of the hospital with mysterious symptoms related to his heart. Coach Daniels allowed me miss practice one weekend to go check on him.

The instant I arrived at the hospital, I regretted having gone at all. It was hard to see a man as strong as my dad relegated to a hospital bed. The image of my dad being weak and feeble plagued me. I knew it was killing my mom, too. Her pain hurt me even more. She tried not to let me see her cry, but the redness in her eyes betrayed her.

Bryce didn't make it any better. Every day when I talked to him, he would tell me how great school was going, and I didn't want to burden him with my troubles. We talked daily more out of habit than anything else. It bothered me that this was where we were, but we made a pact not to complain anymore. The last time he visited me, he gave me a promise ring. Bryce promised that we were going to make it through these college years and that he would be faithful to me and be understanding of my schedule.

This night was like many others where my run led me to the gym. The gym was like a sanctuary for me. It was filled with serenity and peace. I loved having the gym all to myself at night. It felt like the game belonged to me and only me again. I put up several hundred shots and then emulated the end of a game with the moon shining on me. I was the commentator, the coach, and the player. Narrating the game, calling and making plays. I did this until I began to see the twilight outside. In those few moments, I forgot everything. The only thing that mattered was the game.

Later that day, I was in my Math 101 class when my phone buzzed. I fumbled it trying to take it out of my pocket. Deep inside, I was scared something was wrong with my dad, because usually no one texted me that early. I had already spoken to Bryce that morning. He had given me some disappointing news, telling me he wasn't going to be able to make it to my game that night because he had a project he had to finish. When I looked at my phone, I thought I was dreaming. I blinked a few times and asked the guy sitting next to me to read the name just to make sure I wasn't crazy. It was Carter. I hadn't spoken to Carter since I left for school. There were probably at least a hundred times I picked up the phone to call but never pressed send. Most times it was in the middle of the night when I was running or sitting alone in the gym, but I always thought better of it. Rationalizing that he was sleeping or that he was busy—sometimes thinking that our friendship was a thing of the past and something I needed to grow out of.

When I opened the text message, I didn't know what to expect. It simply read, "Good luck Mackenzie! Do your thing girl." I couldn't suppress the smile spreading across my face. I probably read that message forty times before I looked at it one last time when we had to turn our phones in at our pre-game meal about four hours before game time.

Coach Daniels said he took our phones because you had to be fully present to win. As a team we had to focus. In a world full of distractions, it is easy to be in two places at once. One of his biggest pet peeves was if we were at dinner but on our phones and, while we were physically at the table, our minds and hearts were somewhere else, he said.

It is difficult to be fully present in any one place. Social media makes us want to know what is happening somewhere else. It makes us want to know what celebrities are doing, what our friends and family members are doing. These things make it hard to be present in the moment, which in turn makes it nearly impossible to give your all to the task at hand.

The power of being fully present in any moment should never be overlooked. When you are able to "lock in," you become capable of performing at a much higher level and are able to get more out of your relationships, Coach Daniels would say. This ability to be locked in or focused on the task at hand separates the good from the great. It is like using a laser to focus on one particular detail rather than taking on the world all at once.

Finally, it was time for tip-off in my first college game. I found myself somewhere I had never been before during tip-off: on the bench. I quickly found my mom and brother in the stands. My dad's absence was magnified by their presence. While I wanted to be a great teammate and accept my role, my confidence was crushed, and I slightly resented Coach Daniels. I had grown to love the man. He was teaching me so much, and he was completely understanding of my home situation, but I felt like he was taking a bit of revenge on me. I did everything he asked. I worked just as hard as—if not harder than— anyone on the team. But that didn't seem to matter. The longer I sat on the bench, the more these thoughts of doubt and bitterness consumed me.

But with three minutes left in the first half and with a twenty-point lead, he called my name. I played a bit more in the second half and performed decently, but not great. After the game, my mom and Kam greeted me and told me I did great. Then I heard a very familiar voice say "Don't lie to her. That was the worst game I've ever seen her play." It was Carter. I ran and wrapped my arms around him. I could always count on C-Rey to be honest, if nothing else. I couldn't believe he was there. It was the first time I had seen him in months. He looked different. I couldn't exactly say what it was about him that was different, but it was different.

My mom, Kam, and Carter took me to dinner. After dinner, my mom and Kam headed back home. My mom had to get back to my dad. Turner was only a two-and-a-half-hour drive from where I lived. Carter told me he had originally planned on going home, too, but he was going to stay the weekend because he had to "get my mind right" after what he had just witnessed. He asked if he could stay with me and if I would take him to the nearest mall in the morning so he could get some clothes. I told him he could stay but that I had practice in the morning. I offered to give him directions to the mall if he didn't want to wait. I knew he probably had homework, too, back home, but I was glad he was staying.

That night we stayed up talking for a long time until we finally fell asleep. He asked me what was going on. He said my mom had told him about my dad and asked me why I hadn't told him. I could tell he was genuinely hurt that I hadn't. He told me that my pain was his pain and that I should tell him everything. There would be no judgment. I didn't have to be strong or hard for him—or with him. How had I forgotten that?

He wondered aloud to me. And for the first time, I told someone what I was going through. It came out like a flood that had just broken through a dam. I told him how my dad being in the hospital was taking a serious toll on me and how I felt I needed to be strong for my mom. I told him how Bryce just didn't get it. I told him about Coach Daniels and how coming off the bench made me feel like I wasn't good enough to play at this level. I told him how the game had changed and how for the upperclassmen the game seemed so transactional. I told him how it felt corporate and that this wasn't the game I loved. I was overcome with emotion. Carter just held me.

Carter somehow knew exactly what to say. He told me he was proud of me. He said that I shouldn't worry about coming off the bench. He told me to put my pride away, because I was still a very important part of the team. He told me to be confident in that and to play my hardest—whether I played two minutes or forty minutes. He asked if I loved my teammates, and I said yes. I really did love the people I played with. I even loved my coaches. So he told me to play for them. I needed to focus, to play my game, and to have fun. No one can take the game from you, he told me. No one. So don't let them.

I finally found the courage to ask Carter

why he had come after we hadn't spoken in so long. And he made me laugh. He said, "Girl, you know I wouldn't miss it. All the work I put in with you. I had to see your first game. Plus, I had to save our friendship." I don't remember where the conversation ended after that. All I know is that I passed out. It was the first night in a very long time that I actually slept through the night.

6 CONSISTENCY

We were on the road in Memphis for our first away game, five games into the season. We were 4–1. My roommate for the trip was Lauren Grater. LG was my closest friend on the team. She was a senior, and she had taken me under her wing. She wasn't just a friend, either: She was a mentor. Most people said that LG was Turner's best player. She was our leading scorer. She led the team in assists as well, which is pretty special—considering most shooting guards don't get many assists. But if you knew her, that wouldn't surprise you because of how selfless she was. She was always looking out for the younger players. She would take us to the grocery store to get snacks or run us off campus to get food when the cafeteria was closed.

We made up dance routines almost daily. Today wasn't any different, because we were in a nice hotel. Our dance session was interrupted by a deep knock on our hotel door. Lauren opened the door; it was one our coaches who said we were too loud. We both just busted out laughing and apologized. LG and I were both extremely goofy. We turned down the music. There were more knocks on the door. This time I answered the door, "Sorry coach!" I said, but it was all of our teammates. They said they heard we were having a party. Our room was packed with all of the thirteen players spread throughout the room. We plotted how we would sneak out of the hotel the next night after the game to go hang out on Beale Street until the coaches did the room check and everyone returned to their own rooms.

After everyone left, it was time to go to sleep. I lay in my bed awake. I didn't know how quickly LG would fall asleep. "LG," I called out. "What's up Mack?" Lauren replied in a muffled voice from her side of the room. "Are you sleep?" I asked. She replied with a bit of sarcasm, "I could be if you weren't talking to me." I debated whether or not to ask the question that was burning inside of me. I looked up Lauren's bio on our team website and learned that she had barely played her freshman and sophomore years, but now she was a freaking beast. I wanted to know what changed. Since Carter came, I was playing with a lot better focus and was feeling much more positive.

I still yearned to reach that next level. I decided I didn't take myself seriously enough to be afraid to look silly, so I asked, "LG, what was the turning point for you? How did you go from averaging six or seven points a game to eighteen last year and, not sure where you are this year, but you did hit thirty-four two days ago?" I could hear LG rustling and turning over as if she were fighting with the covers. She finally sat up on the edge of the bed and replied, "I had to figure out how to be consistent. Coach Daniels would always be so frustrated with me my freshman year because he said I had a ton of potential but that I only played when I felt like it.'"

"I don't know man, I just want to do whatever takes to help us win. I don't want to wait until I'm a senior," I said. She replied, "Mack, you are on the right track. You've definitely gotten better every game. What I would say is whatever it is that you do well, do it all the time. Be consistent. It is difficult to find people who can be counted on. It is even harder to find people who do what they say they are going to do when they say they are going to do it. If you can do those things, you will automatically be above average, because the average person does not follow through, and the average person's word means very little. Consistency is even on a bad night bringing that thing to the table that only you can. Consistency is being reliable, it is showing up. Consistency is rare. Therefore, consistency is valued highly." Lauren was always going below the surface. She led the Fellowship of Christian Athletes at Turner, and she was a master at relating things to the bigger picture. I loved that about Lauren.

"Why is it so hard to be consistent?" I asked. Lauren said, "Consistency is difficult because of feelings and emotions. Feelings and emotions cause us to act differently based on our mood that current day. Also, as individuals, we struggle to replicate the energy and effort from day to day because we perform according to what we feel rather than at our best. Don't let outside circumstances dictate your day-to-day performance. When you allow things that you can't control determine your level of effort or your attitude, you have been defeated. This is why it is important to be grounded in the knowledge of who you are and whose you are. When you know those two things, you know that all that is required of you each day is that you do your very best and that, little by little, as you consistently do your best, you will improve, and the people around you will be blessed by the gifts God placed in you." I was sure LG was going to be some sort of counselor or psychiatrist. She claimed she was going to be a physical therapist, but she changed her mind every week. I knew whatever profession she ended up in she was going to be a blessing to everyone around her.

7 PLAY TO WIN

It was five o'clock in the morning, and Kirk Franklin was blaring on my stereo. My morning gospel playlist always seemed to get me ready for the day ahead. I had a huge final exam that day in Psychology. This test was worth sixty percent of my grade in the class. I had spent the last week working with my tutors on memorizing every piece of information from the semester. Sigmund Freud's and Abraham Maslow's theories were dancing around my brain. Easton's semester wrapped up a few days before ours did, so Bryce volunteered to come help me study as well. I told him he would be more of a distraction than a help, but he insisted on coming. He made me flash cards and drilled me on them every night after I had met with the tutors.

I got up early, because I figured I could cram in another couple of hours of studying before going to the exam at 8 AM. I didn't wake Bryce, because he looked like he was sleeping well, and him not moving at all with my stereo blasting confirmed it. Around 6:45, I finished studying, jumped in the shower, and got dressed. Bryce still wasn't awake. I grabbed my pencil and my notes and headed to the cafeteria for breakfast. I wanted to get to the test a few minutes early to ask the teacher a question before the test began. On my way to the cafeteria, my phone rang. It was Carter.

"Good morning, Carter," I answered. "What's up, Mackenzie?" he replied.

"Just getting ready to go take this final exam, and I hope I don't fail," I said.

"You won't." said Carter. "Okay, I trust you. Plus Bryce is here and has been helping me study, so I feel good about this test. How were your finals?" I asked him. "They came and went. My last one was yesterday. Now I'm just waiting for you to come home for Christmas," he said.

"Me too. I need a break. I'll be home after my game next Monday. So that's six days away. Are you coming to the game? We play

Rachel's team. They are undefeated, so it should be a good game. Rachel has been playing like Shaq, your girl is killing it." I laughed a little as I said the last part.

"That's not my girl!" he said emphatically. I knew I would get a rise out of him. "Didn't you have a thing for her junior year?" I asked. "No, I didn't," he said with a finality that meant that discussion was over. "Are you going to come to the game?" I asked. Carter had been to a few of my games since the first one, but this was the first time I asked him to come. "Is Bryce going to stay for your game?" he asked.

"Yes."

"That will be his first time seeing you play in college, right?"

"Yes." I said knowing exactly what was coming next.

"Nah, I'll pass. Bryce won't want me there."

"Why do you think that?" I asked.

"I don't think it, I know it. I'll just try to catch up with you when you get home," he said.

The next few days went by quickly. I was excited to play against one of my good friends. Rachel had been my teammate for the last eight years in both AAU and school basketball. Now, she would be on the other team, trying to block my shot. We were both ultra-competitive, which is why I think we got along so well. I mean, we competed in everything, from basketball to school to who could eat their food the fastest. With us, everything was a competition. I think playing for my dad made us that way.

He would always tell us that there is only one way to play the game—and that is to win the game. Any other way is an insult to the game and an even bigger insult to the opponent. The thing that separates Michael Jordan and Kobe Bryant from everyone else who has ever played the game is their competitiveness. Competitiveness is the will to win. The drive to compete and push past any perceived barriers to reach the ultimate goal. It is competition that makes the game worth playing. What most people don't realize is that the greatest competition of all is the competition against one's self. The ability to channel inner competition is the greatest secret to success. If every day you compete to be better than you were yesterday, you will grow and develop exponentially and achieve great success along the way.

The greatest teammates are not the ones who pat you on the back and act like a cheerleader. The great teammates are the ones who in practice will push you to get better. They push you to exceed your limits. They take every drill as a competition and play to win as if something is always on the line which is why Rachel was always my greatest teammate. Even though we played different positions, we always pushed each other to get better.

Tonight Rachel and I were not teammates—we were enemies. Rachel's team ended up winning the game by one point on a buzzer beater. I took all losses hard. I hate to lose. It cut me deeply when my team lost, whether I played well or not. This loss pierced me to the core, because I knew I would not hear the end of it. Especially since we were all riding home together after the game. Bryce tried to make me feel better, but all he did was frustrate me. "It's just a game, Mackenzie" he said. We didn't speak the rest of the way home.

8 TALENT MEANS NOTHING

The seniors, LG, Ty, and even Kaylen, who, for the first time appeared to be a human being, were all sitting at their lockers crying. I was in complete shock. March Madness was over for us in the first round. We were a 4- seed and got upset by a 13-seed that had only won 12 games this season. We had won 20 games. How did this happen? Coach Daniels was livid. He kept repeating something but I was not paying much attention because I still couldn't believe that we had lost. Then he took the white board marker and wrote on the board, "There is nothing more common than unsuccessful men with talent— Calvin Coolidge"; he underlined it profusely and stormed out of the locker room. It's true. We had played like crap. Had we underestimated our opponent?

I just watched the seniors. They were not crying silently. Their cries were loud and their tears ran down their faces like a glass tipped over at dinner. I felt like I was invading their privacy, but I couldn't look away. LG in particular held my attention. I knew we had let her down, and my stomach twisted in large knots at the thought. I could only imagine how she felt. They didn't have another chance at playing college basketball, and this last performance was not even worthy of being called a performance. I made a mental note to leave everything on the court every chance I get, because I didn't ever want the feeling that I was witnessing. I got dressed and prepared my apology to my mom, Kam, and Carter, who had come to my game. They had been a great support for me all season. My mom had been a trooper— not missing a game—which was amazing considering the condition my dad was in. He hadn't made a game all year, which was a whole new experience for me. I was still getting used to not having him bark at me from the sidelines and for hours after the game.

I'm not quite sure if I was processing the fact that my freshman season was over. I was a bit numb to it. They always say that anything can happen on any given day, but I never really paid much attention to it. I had looked past this game because I had assumed it would be an easy win for us; I was ready for a rematch against Rachel's team, which we would get if both of our teams won the first round of the NCAA tournament. After I talked to my family, I put on my noise-canceling headphones and took that dreadful walk to the bus. The whole way to the airport, Adele, Drake, and Anita Baker sang to me. It was a pretty somber ride. Bryce and Carter both texted me, but I didn't text back because I always hated to lose, but it was killing me that we had lost to a team that was not better than us. It was eating away at me that we had to wait another eight months before we would get to play again. Another eight months before we could prove we are better than what we had just displayed. Another eight months and we still will never be able to make it up to LG, Ty, and Kaylen.

9 INSTINCT COMES FROM REPITTION

Over the course of the summer, my father's health grew worse. I stayed away on purpose. I was a coward. I couldn't stand to see my father like that. I was great at making up excuses for not coming home. I also had summer school and workouts, which largely helped me avoid the topic. I talked to my mom every day. She was so strong. I truly admired her faith in God and how she seemed to balance being a good mom and wife while running her own business. I never knew how much we struggled until I left for college and saw what my mom had to deal with when my dad wasn't able to go to work. Somehow she was still able to keep everything in order with just her salary and the little help my brother could provide from his start up. He had offered many times to go get a desk job to help my mom, but she refused. She wanted Kam to follow his dreams and knew that he was going to be successful no matter what he did.

I would never admit it but part of the reason I didn't want to be home was because of Carter. I wanted to talk to C-Rey, he was the only one I wanted to talk to, but I couldn't bring myself to do it. He had a new girlfriend. He didn't even tell me about her. I found out when he brought her to my brother's birthday dinner. She was pretty. Her name was Blair. She was a little bit older than Carter. I think she had recently graduated from college. I don't believe she liked me too much, but that could be my imagination. The two weeks I was home, the only time I saw Carter was at my brother's dinner, which had never happened before. I usually saw Carter almost every day. Bryce didn't really like that Carter and I hung out so much, but it was never something that I was willing to give up. I think Bryce knew it too, because he never forced the issue. So, I just pretended like I didn't see Bryce flinch every time I mentioned Carter's name. I guess this was a part of the maturation process. No one thought our friendship could or would last as long as it did. They said it wasn't sustainable. Maybe they were right.

Our friendship had always come so naturally, though. We were in the seventh grade, and I knew who Carter was because who didn't know who Carter was? He was the best basketball player at our school, and he knew he was. One day after school on the playground there was a pickup game, and I was the only girl there trying to play with the guys. Carter was the first captain, and with his first pick he said, "I've got the girl." I didn't think anyone had even noticed me at the back of the pack. There were at least twenty guys standing in front of me. My plan was just to wait a few games until I could be the captain, which was usually the only way I could get on the court. This time Carter Reyes picked me. We ran the court. No matter who got on the court, the game was over before it ever started. There was just no way you could beat us together. It was something to see. You would have thought we had been playing together for years—our chemistry was ridiculous. His confidence to not just pick me but pick me first made me play like a maniac. I wanted to prove him right. My best games always came with Carter as my teammate or front row. From the seventh grade until now we had been a team, and nothing had ever come between that team. Even when I didn't believe in our team, Carter always did and kept the team together.

Without Carter, I had to teach Bryce how to be my teammate. Bryce did his best to act like he enjoyed coming to the gym with me. But it wasn't the same. It wasn't fun anymore. I knew I shouldn't compare, but going to the gym with Bryce was like shooting baskets at Dave and Buster's. It felt like the goal was constantly moving. I tried to talk to my dad about it, and he told me it was like instincts in basketball. Instincts come from repetition, and repetition develops confidence. He said that I had had more reps with Carter and that if I didn't put the reps in, then I wouldn't have the confidence. I had to learn to trust Bryce. I had to forget about Carter. It was time to let go of the playground game and embrace the corporate game. It was time to grow up. It was time to go to work.

Part 2

10 BE GRATEFUL

My greatest fear for my senior year had turned into my reality my senior year. The game had become very transactional for me. I showed up when I supposed to. I laced up my sneakers and put on my Turner uniform. I smiled for the fans. I was quietly being smothered by the responsibilities associated with the game. I felt enslaved. It was no longer a game. It was a job.

On our first day of conditioning in August, we went to the football field to do our conditioning test. I had made all of my times so far, and now it was time for the last sprint. I was feeling good. I had a lot of adrenaline going because if I made this last sprint, I wouldn't have to do any "voluntary" breakfast club conditioning, which everyone had to do until they passed the conditioning test. I stepped to the line with a ton of confidence because in my fourth year of doing this, I had learned how to pace myself to have enough energy to finish strong. The whistle blew, and I took off. I was easily at least five or six yards of ahead of everyone. I heard my coaches cheering my teammates and me on.

I chopped my feet as I approached the line. I planted my foot to turn and went and stepped on a rock. I heard the crack and fall to the ground. I was writhing in pain. I clutched my left ankle with both hands. I tasted blood in my mouth. I must have bit my tongue as I hit the ground. My entire body was numb. It felt like an eternity, but within seconds I was surrounded by my teammates, coaches, and trainer. The trainer made all of my teammates walk away. I was fighting back tears. I didn't want anyone to see me cry. A few tears escaped anyway. I wasn't crying so much because of the pain; I could feel that my career was over. The game had been stolen from me.

In that moment, I was quickly and sternly humbled. How arrogant had I been to think that everything I had couldn't be taken away. To believe that there was something uniquely special about me. I'd never been injured before. I thought I was invincible. It was confirmed that I had broken my ankle and that I would be out for the next couple of months. I had surgery scheduled for the end of the week. My mom was coming down for the surgery. Bryce wanted to come, but I told him not to. I didn't like him seeing me weak or vulnerable.

I watched workouts for a week, and I wanted to pull my hair out. The hardest part of being injured wasn't using the crutches or wearing the boot. It wasn't the massive swelling in my ankle. The pain wasn't really that terrible, either, because I was popping pills like candy. The hardest part was watching other people play the game and not being able to play if I wanted to. The whole week leading up to my surgery, all I did was watch practice, go to class, and sleep. I wasn't in the mood to talk to anyone.

The night before my surgery, while my mom was sleeping I called an Uber to pick me up from my apartment and take me to campus. I crutched out of the apartment without waking my mom, because I knew if she woke up she wouldn't let me go. I went straight to the locker room to find my high tops and a basketball. It was really hard to crutch with the ball in my hands, so

I had to pick one. I left the crutches. I hobbled out to center court, holding on to my basketball like a hug that lingers with a dear friend you've been away from too long. I stood there for a long time, broken and humbled. I had taken the game for granted. The only friend who had stood by me through everything, and I just wanted to be forgiven.

11 YOU ARE NEVER OUT OF THE FIGHT

I woke up in the cold hospital room after my surgery. I was groggy from all the medication. For the most part, I was numb—my ankle from the surgery and subsequent pain pills and the rest of my body from the cold, with the exception of my right hand which was warm. The warmth was coming from someone's hand, but it wasn't my mother's. It was too rough. I didn't have a lot of energy, but I managed to turn my head around, and I laid eyes on Carter. I didn't know whether to be pissed or jubilant. I hadn't seen Carter in two years. Every time I came home, he was "too busy" to hang out and he didn't answer my calls. So I stopped calling.

"Why are you here? Who told you? Where is Blair?" The questions came like a waterfall of venom. By the way Carter clinched his jaw, I could tell that my tone and questions stung him, but he didn't loosen his grip on my hand—and I didn't pull away either.

"Well, Mackenzie," he said slowly, as if he was calculating his every word. He paused and took a deep breath. "I thought why I was here was obvious. I'm here for you. Rachel told me you were here." I had to process the fact that C-Rey could take Rachel's calls, but he couldn't take mine. "And lastly, Blair is back home," he said. This told me they were still together.

"I'm sure she wouldn't like you being here. Maybe it is best if you leave," I said, trying to find the resolve to rip my hand from his.

"I'm not leaving, Mackenzie, especially not when your mom is gone to get some food. Mama Moore would kill me if I left her baby in the hospital alone," he said. His grip on my hand got tighter as he said this.

"I'm going to have to talk to my mom about leaving me in the care of strangers," I said.

"She wouldn't have to leave you with strangers if Bryce was here. Where is Bryce exactly?" It was Carter's turn to throw punches.

"I told Bryce not to come." I was ready to go toe-to-toe with Carter when the doctor came into the room. He asked me how I was feeling, gave me some general instructions, and gave me my prescriptions for the pain.

We grabbed some Chick-Fil-A and my medication on the way to my apartment. I didn't want Bryce to come, but my mom said I was being unreasonable. I didn't have the energy to fight it. I was too doped up. I fell asleep soon after we got home. I woke up in severe pain. I suppose my medication had worn off. I let out a shriek. Carter came running into my room to check on me. And I saw it for the first time—he was truly concerned. It was written all over his face. He went and got my pain medicine and water and sat there with me until I fell asleep again.

At the end of the weekend, my mother had to return home to work and my dad. Kam was looking after my dad but had to go back to work on Monday. Carter had to leave to go back to school, too. He told me he was going to be back on Thursday and stay for the rest of the weekend. I protested, and on the whole didn't treat him very well while he was there. He told me no matter what I said, I couldn't keep him away, and he was going to come every weekend until I got back to one-hundred percent. Carter was very resilient. You had to love that about him. Part of me wanted him to be there, because I knew the journey to recovery was going to be excruciating, and I would need his resilience. I needed my bounce-back game to be strong.

Every time I watched my teammates work out, I yearned to be back. Then, I would hit my cast against a wall and remember how difficult it was going to be to come back from this. Would I even be the same once I was finished rehabbing? Should I take the red shirt and come back for a fifth year? Coach Daniels had asked me about the red shirt at least fifty times, but I felt like it was a cop out. I couldn't wait that long to play again. I needed to be back on the court yesterday. I couldn't even start my rehab until I got out of the hard cast in about four to six weeks. I was already tired of the crutches, although I had grown attached to my scooter. I even named my scooter; his name was Riley.

I was surprised when I got home on Thursday night and Carter was waiting for me. I didn't think he would actually come, especially after how I had treated him the last weekend. But there he was, just sitting outside my apartment, smiling at me. I just shook my head, unlocked the door, and crutched in without saying a word. He followed me in and put his duffel bag by the couch. I went to my room and closed the door. I fell on the bed, laughed to myself, and proceeded to put my face in a pillow and scream. How did he find his way back into my life? My pride wouldn't let me talk to him. I had a feeling this was a battle I was going to lose, but I wasn't going to give in easy. I had so much anger concealed within in me. I felt betrayed. But it was a lot of work being mad at Carter. In all the years we had been friends, we never had had a real fight, and we could never be mad at one another. It just didn't happen. And now here I was really trying to be upset.

C-Rey was doing everything right. He cooked for me, he brought me my medicine, and made sure my ankle was always elevated. He would go to the Redbox, and we would sit in silence and watch movies all day. He would drive me anywhere I needed to go. He never looked for a thank you, although I did at least always manage to tell him thank you. He never pressured me to talk. He knew I was upset and just let me be. I was grateful for that. He knew we would talk when I was ready. To a certain extent, I feel like he was trying to exorcise his own demons. I could tell he was disappointed in himself for letting me down. Maybe he missed me too, but I couldn't tell just yet.

We went on like this every Thursday night to Monday morning for weeks. I video chatted with Bryce everyday but hadn't seen him in person since right before school started. I kept putting him off when he wanted to come on the weekends. I couldn't tell him that Carter had been coming on the weekends. Secretly, Bryce was probably happy about Carter's disappearing act. Bryce and I were in a really good place and not arguing anymore. I didn't want to mess it up if I wasn't sure Carter and I would reconcile. I hated arguing with Bryce.

12 DELAYED GRATIFICATION

My first week out of the cast and working with the physical therapist in rehab was brutal. I contemplated quitting at least seventeen times that I can vividly remember. The therapist told me that my range of motion had to improve substantially before I'd be able to play again. I was in a boot but still had to use the crutches because I wasn't ready to put consistent pressure on my ankle. I wasn't healing fast enough.

Thursday after rehab, Carter picked me up, and we went home. I walked into the house and took my boot off. I tried to walk without putting enough pressure on my hurt ankle to feel it. I was determined to walk from the door to the couch. It hurt like hell. I gritted my teeth, grimacing in pain, and tried to push through it. Somehow I ended up on the ground and never made it to the couch. Carter came over to me with a bag of ice and a pillow. Out of frustration, I punched the couch over and over and over until Carter grabbed my fist and pulled me into his chest. "It is a process; trust the process," he said. "I know you are frustrated, but you will win if you don't quit."

The dam between my brain and my mouth finally broke. "Where have you been? It's been two years. Now every time I see you, I think you are going to leave. You just stopped being there. I know it was Blair. You chose her over me. We were supposed to be best friends."

"We are best friends. That never changed. We didn't talk, and I'll admit that is my fault. I apologize. Blaming Blair isn't fair. Blair is just closer than you are, and she likes to spend every free minute together. She doesn't like for me to be on my phone around her. And I thought I was in love with her, so I wanted to make her happy."

"So does she know you have been coming here every weekend?" I asked.

"Umm, not exactly. I mean kinda. Just not every weekend. Does Bryce know I'm here every weekend? You know he hates me."

"Nope. I still don't believe you are here," I said.

"Well you better believe because I'm not going anywhere, and you can't get rid of me."

"We'll see about that."

"Seriously, though. I hated missing your games. I watched them all online, but it's not the same. It would have been too cool being at your first twenty-point game. I knocked my laptop off my desk and almost broke my laptop when you hit that step back three."

"You watched my games?" I asked in shock, not feeling as alone as I had four minutes ago.

"Every single one. But let's get on the rehab. Where is your stretchy band?"

"It's in my back pack." The rest of the night, we did my home rehab exercises and talked. We laughed—the kind of laugher that comes from deep within your soul. It was like we picked up where we had left off two years ago. He was him and I was me and we were us again.

The next few weeks, I became super close with my trainer and physical therapist. I was determined not to be defeated. Every time I got down on myself, I had to remember that this was a journey and that I had to love the process. I'd never been injured before, so it was a new journey for me. Kam would send me these little motivational videos each morning, and, though I wouldn't tell him, they helped. One video he sent me talked about delayed gratification. It stuck with me because it talked about putting a demand on greatness through the work that you do. When you put the work in, greatness has no choice but to come. By no means is it easy though. The process hurt. The process was designed to break you down and build you up in such a way that you would be worthy of the greatness. Throughout my rehab, I knew there would come a tipping point where things would finally start going my way. I was ready for that point to come. Carter, who pushed me even harder than my trainers and cared for me in way that I would never be able to repay him for, would tell me, "It's coming; just wait on it and while you are waiting, attack it."

13 ENERGY AND ENTHUSIASM

In *Lone Survivor*, one of the soldiers says, "Anything worth doing is worth overdoing. Moderation is for cowards." I was ready to overdo everything. I was overjoyed when I left the doctor's office and was cleared to play. After an extended period of rehab and a couple of setbacks, I was finally released. It was mid-season, and my coaches were starting to think I wouldn't be back at all. I called my mom, and she was so excited for me. Now, I had to figure out how I was going to go all the way until Thursday to tell Carter that I cleared. I wanted to tell him in person. I thought Carter deserved that. He didn't know that I had a doctor's appointment that week. I was nervous I wouldn't get cleared, and the last time I didn't get cleared, he tried to hide it, but I know he was devastated.

When I told Bryce, he wanted to come down for the weekend. I quickly told him no. He was trying to figure out why. He just wanted to celebrate with me. I had been telling him he couldn't come on the weekends for months. I'd seen him only once or twice. I told him since he didn't have class on Wednesday's that would be a good day to visit. I had used every excuse I could think of for why he couldn't come on the weekends. I don't even know why I felt like couldn't tell him Carter was coming. It wasn't like I was cheating on Bryce, but I think he would think I was.

It was an indescribable feeling being back on the court with my teammates. I was a little rusty, but I brought it every day. The energy was contagious. Our practices were fun to me for the first time in years. Even Coach Daniels, who could be overly serious from time to time, seemed to be enjoying himself. I think it helped that our team had been winning. My teammates were playing phenomenally. I was so excited just to be a part of it and play whatever role I could to help the team. Coach said once I was ready I'd go back to starting, and I told coach that I didn't mind coming off the bench if that is what the team needed me to do. I was grateful for every second.

Other than practice, the days dragged by until Thursday finally came. I made sure I got all my studying done in advance so I would have time to cook for C-Rey before he arrived on Thursday. I just wanted to do something nice to show my appreciation. I couldn't wait to tell him the good news—especially since my first game back was going to be on Friday at home, and he would be able to see it. My mom, dad, and Kam were going to come down. It would be the first time my dad actually got to see me play college ball in person. He was getting stronger.

When Carter arrived, I couldn't hold it in for very long. I was giddy. As soon as he walked through the door, I told him. He just smiled really big, picked me up, and spun me around. He was stronger than I remembered, and he smelled very good. He must have gotten a new cologne. Or maybe I had just never noticed before.

"Mackenzie is back! Let's go!" he said when he finally put me down. He was fired up.

"I'm back," I said.

"I'm glad, because now I can stop being nice to you all the time and beat you up when you are a jerk and start talking crazy," he said, giving me a little jab. We started to play fight and wrestle in the living room. It was pretty back and forth until I started talking trash. Then it got a little more serious, and he over-powered me. Carter had me pinned to the ground, straddling me, out of breath, just looking at me. I saw something in his eyes that I had never seen before. I just started laughing while trying to figure out what it was that was happening. Then I heard the door knob to my apartment turn. Bryce walked in the apartment, looked from me to Carter, drew his own conclusions, and stormed out. I jumped up to go after him. I couldn't figure out how he had gotten in. He must have kept my spare key from when he had helped me move in. I could never find my spare. I always figured it would turn up sooner or later. And it had in a very big and destructive way. I had to find a way to fix it.

I finally caught up to Bryce. He was furious. Bryce was a big guy, so when he got upset he was very demonstrative, using his hands and grabbing his head a lot.

"I always knew it," he said.

"Knew what, Bryce?" I asked, trying not to sound patronizing; but I knew where this conversation was going, and it was one we had had many times before.

"That you have been cheating on me with

Carter this whole time. For all of the almost six years we have been together. Six years," he said, putting up the number six with his fingers for emphasis.

"I've never cheated on you, Bryce. Carter is my friend. He is my best friend."

"I thought you guys stopped talking a long time ago."

"We did, but we started back."

"When?"

"After I hurt my ankle."

He started pacing back and forth. I knew he was putting everything together. I just waited for all the fall out. I knew I hadn't done what he was accusing me of, but I had kept him in the dark about this for months. I had kept him away for a long time so I could spend time with Carter.

"It all makes sense now. You didn't want me to come visit you because of him."

"It's not like that. There was a lot going on. I needed space to figure it all out. I didn't know if Carter and I would be able to pick up where we left off."

"Looks like you guys are doing just fine— and then some. Mackenzie, if you don't want to be with me just say so. I've tried to do everything you have asked me to do. I've been here. I don't know what more you want. I'll never be him, which means I'll never be good enough."

"You are good enough, Bryce. You always have been."

"Mackenzie, we are lying to ourselves, and you know it. This is just comfortable and easy. I can't do it anymore. I'm done. You should have more than enough space now."

"Bryce, don't be like that."

"It's over. Give me my ring back."

I walked past my apartment replaying what Bryce had said over and over again in my head. Was it true? I was sad, but I wasn't disappointed about the break up. The truth was, we had broken up long ago but kept the title. I was numb to it, but I felt like a weight had been lifted off of me. When I finally went back to my apartment Carter wanted to talk, but I hadn't processed what had just happened, and we pretty much ate in silence until I went to sleep. Carter said he had something he wanted to tell me, but I asked him if we could talk about it the next day after the game.

Carter and I never talked after the game.

Bryce ended up coming to my game, which was only the sixth or seventh game he had seen me play in college. Bryce grabbed me when I came out of the locker room. I could see Carter in the distance watching us talk. Bryce gave me a very adamant apology and insisted that I take the ring back. I didn't want it, but I was so confused that I took it. I told him we could go to dinner after I talked to my family and Carter. I went to talk to my family but couldn't find Carter anywhere. I figured he had just gone back to my apartment.

14 CLIQUE

On my way to dinner, I thought about all the time I had invested in my relationship with Bryce. I thought about how our families had pretty much already planned our wedding. I thought about how we were when we first started dating, and I thought about how we were now. I knew I loved Bryce, and I knew he loved me. We looked great together in pictures, and on paper were a perfect match.

Then I thought about my team and how Coach Daniels was always telling us that there was nothing more important than the people that you spend your time with. He would tell us that teams perform so much better when you enjoy being around each other. He talked about how iron sharpens iron and that the people around you should make you better—they should lift you up. They should cover your flaws and amplify your strengths. And I thought to myself: would I want Bryce on my team? Could Bryce be my teammate?

Did Bryce make me better? Did Bryce believe in my dreams? I couldn't answer definitively at that moment. I wanted to ask him. I needed to know. He hadn't been there at the times I needed him, but I couldn't blame him completely for that. I had kept him at a distance. But why had I done that?

At dinner, we talked. Well, he talked mostly. All I heard him talk about was his future and how he wanted me at his side. I interrupted him.

"Bryce, what did you think of my game? Did I look like myself?" I asked.

"Yeah, of course, you did great, Sweetheart," he said. I thought to myself, wow, because I felt like I was rusty. I brought a lot of energy and didn't play bad, but he had no idea.

"Really?" I asked.

"Yes, really. You know I don't get into all that basketball stuff. You only have a few more games left anyway. You really need to start thinking about other things," he said.

"Hmm. Okay," I said. I was little upset with that comment but was going to let it go. My phone was ringing, and Carter was calling. I tried to shut the screen off but Bryce saw it anyway.

"What is his deal anyway? I've never understood why you guys are so close. He likes you. You know that, right?" Bryce said. I thought back to the night before and the way that Carter had looked at me. No one had ever looked at me that way before. It all finally clicked for me.

"I need to go, Bryce. I'm sorry, but you were right yesterday. We are done," I said. I gave him his ring back for a second time.

I raced home, driving like a NASCAR driver, swerving in and out of lanes. I called Carter five times on my way home, but he didn't answer. When I got home, I didn't see Carter's car outside. I just hit my steering wheel a few times, accidentally hitting the horn. I laid my head on the steering wheel. A knock on my window startled me. It was Carter. He had two Redbox movies in hand.

I jumped out of my car and asked, "What do you have to tell me, Carter?"

"It's not important. How was your dinner

with Bryce?" he said.

"It was fine. It's over. I'm done, but I need you to tell me what you wanted to tell me," I said. I noticed the flicker in his eyes. Had he always looked at me like this? I wondered. How could I have missed it?

"I wanted to tell you that I broke up with Blair weeks ago, but I didn't know why I did until yesterday," he said.

"Why did you, C-Rey?" I asked.

"Because I spent all this time trying to turn her into you. She could never be you. And ever since the seventh grade, you are the only girl I have ever wanted on my team," he said. I smiled and hugged him. He lifted me off the ground, and when he looked me in my eyes, I knew it was game over. No one else ever had a chance. I'd been in love with him since the seventh grade and couldn't see it.

ABOUT THE AUTHOR

Amenemopé McKinney is a former Division 1 point guard. She currently coaches girl's high school club basketball. She is the CEO of Ambytion Sports Enterprises in Dallas, TX. She holds an Electrical Engineering degree from Rice University.

Connect with the Author

Twitter

@ambytion_sports

Instagram

@ambytionsports

Website

ambytionsports.com

Made in the USA
San Bernardino, CA
18 February 2016